SANTA'S CHRISTMAS TRAIN

ISBN-13: 978-0-8249-5673-8

Published by Ideals Children's Books
A division of Worthy Media, Inc.
Nashville, Tennessee
www.idealsbooks.com

Library of Congress Cataloging-in-Publication Data
James, Helen Foster, date.
  Santa's Christmas train / written by Helen Foster James ; illustrated by Bill Bolton.
    pages cm
  Summary: Rhyming text follows a group of children as they take a long train
  ride to Santa's Workshop, meet Santa and Mrs. Claus and some elves, receive
  presents, and have their pictures taken before returning home.
    ISBN 978-0-8249-5673-8 (hardcover : alk. paper)
    [1. Stories in rhyme. 2. Trains—Fiction. 3. Christmas—Fiction.
    4. Santa Claus—Fiction.] I. Bolton, Bill, date, illustrator. II. Title.
    PZ8.3.J1477San 2015
    [E]—dc23
                        2015000329

Designed by Georgina Chidlow-Rucker
Printed and bound in China
Leo_Jun15_1

FOR BOB. —H.F.J.

FOR BEN AND AMY. —B.B.

SANTA'S CHRISTMAS TRAIN

Written by

HELEN FOSTER JAMES

Illustrated by

BILL BOLTON

ideals children's books.
Nashville, Tennessee

All Aboard!
Clickety-clack!

Santa's train is
on the track.

TOOT, TOOT, TOOT,
the whistle blows.
Climb aboard
and off it goes.

Up, up, up,

and down, down, down,

through the tunnel,
past our town—

seeing sights
along our way
to see Santa
on his sleigh!

Special snacks
for us tonight.
Minty stripes of
red and white.

Chocolate milk
and cookies too.

Tasty treats for
me and you.

Jingle bells,
we hear them ring.
Christmas carols,
we all sing.

Slowing down,
we've come so far.

Santa's Village—
here we are!

Red and green
are everywhere.
Bells of silver,
here and there.

Twinkling lights
fill up the night.

Decorations
shine so bright!

Mrs. Claus
is fun to see,
lighting up the
Christmas tree.

Helpful elves,
we see them too,
busy doing
what elves do.

"Ho! Ho! Ho!"
and Santa's here,
laughing, waving,
as we cheer.

Santa's sack
is stuffed with toys,
tied with bows for
girls and boys.

Santa says,
"This one's for you!
CHRISTMAS DAY
you'll find some too!"

Strike a pose and
CLICK,
CLICK,
CLICK.

Here's our photo with

SAINT
NICK.

We've had fun,
but now we know,
to the station
we must go.

Up, up, up,

and down, down, down,

through the tunnel,
to our town.

Back at last,
we wave goodbye

Silent night—
it's time to rest.
We like Santa's
train the best!